Zeke Meeks

ARRRRRGH!

HECTOR'S LAME
PUPPET PAL
PIRATE

↓

My best
friend needs
LOTS OF HELP!

Zeke Meeks is published by
Picture Window Books
A Capstone Imprint
1710 Roe Crest Drive
North Mankato, MN 56003
www.capstonepub.com

Copyright ©2012 Picture Window Books

Library of Congress Cataloging in Publication Data
Green, D. L. (Debra L.)
  Zeke Meeks vs. the putrid Puppet Pals / by D. L. Green;
illustrated by Josh Alves.
    p. cm. — (Zeke Meeks)
  Summary: All the children in the third grade except Zeke
Meeks are playing with the newest fad, Puppet Pals finger
puppets—will Zeke give in to the pressure and join them,
even though he would much rather play basketball?
  ISBN 978-1-4048-6803-8 (library binding)
  ISBN 978-1-4048-7223-3 (pbk.)
  1. Finger puppets—Juvenile fiction. 2. Fads—Juvenile fiction.
3. Friendship—Juvenile fiction. 4. Schools—Juvenile fiction.
[1. Finger puppets—Fiction. 2. Puppets—Fiction.
3. Fads—Fiction. 4. Friendship—Fiction. 5. Schools—Fiction.
6. Humorous stories.]
I. Alves, Josh, ill. II. Title. III. Title: Zeke Meeks versus the
putrid Puppet Pals.
  PZ7.G81926Zh 2012
  813.6—dc23   2011029901

Vector Credits: Shutterstock
Book design by K. Fraser

Printed in the United States of America
in Stevens Point, Wisconsin.
022012   006591R

MY DOG AS
A PUPPET PA

↑

...eks

VS THE PUTRID PUPPET PALS

BY
D. L. GREEN

ILLUSTRATED BY
JOSH ALVES

PICTURE WINDOW BOOKS
a capstone imprint

 ← Hawaiian Waggles

TABLE OF

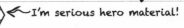 ← I'm serious hero material!

 BOYS RULE EVERYTHING BUT THE PLAYGROUND

vampire finger ⟶

CONTENTS

WOOT!!!!!!!!!!!! My kind of afternoon.

GIRLS DROOL ALL BUT GRACE — SHE BITES

Very, Very, Very Wrong

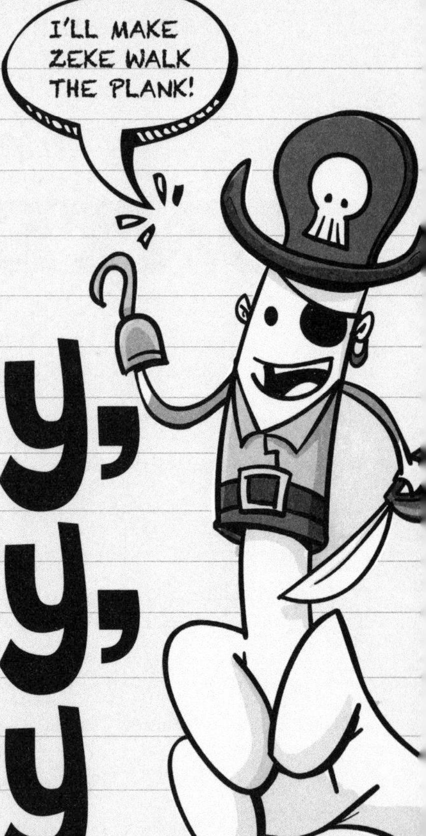

I gasped when I saw Hector Cruz. I knew something was wrong. Very wrong. Very, very wrong. Very, very, very wrong. You get the idea.

Hector Cruz, my best friend, was sitting down during recess. Hector never sat down at recess. Neither did I. At recess we played basketball, soccer, or tag. Sometimes we played all three.

Sometimes we ran away from Nicole Finkle and Buffy Maynard before they could kiss us. But we never sat down.

Owen Leach was sitting next to Hector. This was also very, very, very wrong. Owen Leach also never sat down at recess. He always had kids to play with, because he was the most popular boy in third grade. In fact, there was a waiting list of kids who wanted to play with him.

Owen Leach was much too busy to ever sit down on the playground. Until today.

I rushed over to Hector and Owen. "What happened? Did you break your legs? Should I call for help?" I asked.

They didn't answer me.

I stared at them, trying to figure out what was wrong. The tips of their fingers were bright and colorful.

I said, "You're sitting down at recess, you can't talk, and you have a weird rash on your fingers. Do you have a horrible disease? Were you poisoned?"

Hector finally looked up at me. "Oh, hi, Zeke," he said. "I didn't notice you here. I was busy playing with my new Puppet Pals."

I peered more closely at Hector's and Owen's hands. Those weren't weird rashes on their fingers. Those were felt puppets. I'd seen the commercial for them a lot lately.

Owen started chanting the commercial jingle: "Puppet Pals are so much fun . . ."

Hector joined in, ". . . for just about everyone."

"Who wants to play basketball?" I asked.

"I —" Hector started to say.

"Not us." Owen cut him off. "Puppet Pals are much more popular than basketball." Then he wiggled his index finger, which was covered with a pirate puppet. He said, "Ahoy, matey. Ye olde recess goes great with Puppet Pals."

Hector wiggled his index finger, which had a Puppet Pal ship on it. He said, "All aboard!"

I wasn't aboard. I was just bored. "Are you sure you don't want to play basketball?" I asked.

Owen shook his head.

"No thanks," Hector said.

Owen said, "Zeke, you're disturbing our Puppet Pal time."

I crossed my arms. "Fine," I said. "I'll find someone else to play basketball with."

But it wasn't fine. I wanted to play with Hector, my best friend.

And I couldn't even find anyone to play basketball with. Most of the kids in my third-grade class were playing with their new Puppet Pals.

Nicole Finkle called out, "We'll play with you, Zeke."

"Come over here!" Buffy Maynard yelled.

"Are you going to try to kiss me?" I asked.

Nicole shook her head. "Not today."

"We want to jump rope," Buffy said.

I hadn't jumped rope in a long time. The last time I'd tried, Grace Chang (the meanest girl in school) had tied me to a tree with the rope.

But jumping rope was better than watching people play with finger puppets. So I walked over to Nicole and Buffy.

They each held an end of the rope while I jumped over it. It was fun.

Just as I was thinking that, my feet got
tangled up in the rope. I fell down with the rope
tied around my feet.

"Here's our chance," Nicole said.

"Oh, Zeke, you are so cute," Buffy said.

Then Nicole kissed my right cheek and
Buffy kissed my left cheek.

I felt sick to my stomach. "You said you
wouldn't try to kiss me," I complained.

"We didn't *try* to kiss you," Nicole said.

"You made it so easy for us, we didn't even have to try," Buffy said.

I wiped off my cheeks about a hundred times, rubbed my sick stomach, untangled my feet from the rope, and ran away.

I saw Rudy Morse standing by himself. "Do you want to play basketball?" I asked him.

"No thanks," he said.

DO YOU WANT TO PRACTICE MAKING FART NOISES WITH OUR UNDERARMS?

"I mastered that in second grade," I said.

He frowned. "It's not nice to brag."

"Sorry," I said. "We could do something else together."

"Do you want to practice burping our ABCs?" Rudy asked.

I had mastered that in first grade. But I didn't want to brag. So I said, "I'd rather do something that gets us moving around."

Rudy said, "We can dig in the ground for insects. Yesterday, I found a long, six-legged earwig and a smelly, green stinkbug."

Finding insects sounded even scarier than being kissed by Nicole and Buffy. Insects terrified me. I kept that a secret. I didn't want to get teased.

Rudy bent down and dug under the bushes. He pulled out a giant red beetle.

"I have to go," I said. Then I ran away.

I stopped when I saw Chandler Fitzgerald. He was sitting by himself with his head in his hands.

I said, "Hi, Chandler. Do you want to play basketball?"

A tear fell from his eye. "I'm much too sad to play basketball," he said.

"What's wrong?" I asked.

"Isn't it obvious? If you really cared about me, you'd know what made me so upset," Chandler said. Another tear dripped down his cheek.

"Are you upset about your hair?" I asked. His hair was so greasy it looked wet.

"No." Two more tears plopped onto the playground.

"Are you upset about your nose?" I asked. He had a big red wart on the tip of his nose.

"No." His tears kept coming.

"Are you upset about your voice?" His voice kind of sounded like a broken fiddle — all screechy and stuff.

"No." His tears multiplied.

"I give up. What are you so upset about?"
I asked.

"I have no Puppet Pals!" Tears rushed
down Chandler's face like a giant waterfall,
but not as pretty.

"That's no big deal. Puppet Pals are boring,"
I said.

"Everyone else has them!" Chandler sobbed.

I looked around. Hector and Owen and
almost everyone else in my class were playing
with their Puppet Pals.

I suddenly realized that they were a big
deal. A very big deal.

I had to get some Puppet Pals.

Really, It's Just Dog Drool

SOCKS!!!

Once I got home from school, I plopped down on the couch. Then I frowned. Then I grumbled. Then I punched the pillow. Guess what kind of mood I was in.

Did you guess yet?

Ready?

I'll wait.

I'll wait a bit longer.

ME, MY MOOD, AND I

Okay. If you guessed that I was in "a terrible mood," you're right. Correct answers also include "awful mood," "horrible mood," and "*muy mal humor.*" That last one is Spanish for "very bad mood."

Our dog, Waggles, sat next to me on the couch. He wore a purple, polka-dotted sweater. It looked ridiculous on him. Waggles is a boy. But my sisters and mom always dress him in yucky girly things.

Waggles licked my face to try to cheer me up. Waggles has a giant, squishy tongue. He drools a lot. He's pretty much a champion drooler. If drooling were ever an Olympic sport, Waggles would win a gold medal.

I patted him and said, "I'm sure you meant well. But your drool dripped down my face and got all over my pants."

My younger sister, Mia, came into the room. She pressed the belly button of her Princess Sing-Along doll. The doll started singing a song from the *Princess Sing-Along* TV show.

It was more like screeching than singing. Mia joined in. They screeched, "Make sure to sneeze into your hand, la la la. So you'll know where your snot will land, la la la."

Mia stopped singing.

The Princess Sing-Along doll kept singing. "When you feel sick, stay home from school, la la la. Oozing pus and germs is not cool, la la la."

I pressed hard on the doll's belly button to get it to stop.

"Be nice to Princess Sing-Along," Mia said. Then she pointed to the dog drool on my pants.

"Waggles did that," I said.

"He pee-peed on you?" she asked.

"No," I said.

"That's what I thought. You wet your pants," Mia said.

Before I could explain, Mia said, "Next time you need to tinkle, run to the bathroom." Then she sang another Princess Sing-Along song: "Use the potty. Don't be shy, la la la. Keep your undies nice and dry, la la la."

CUTE BUT ANNOYING

Then she danced away.

My older sister, Alexa, came into the room.

She held a bunch of ugly rubber bracelets.
"I found these bracelets when I was cleaning
out my closet," she said. "They used to be really
popular, but I haven't used them in years. Do
you want them?"

I shook my head.

"You wet your pants. Eww," she said.

I looked down at the big wet spot on my pants. "That's not pee. That's dog drool."

"You have dog drool on your pants. Eww," she said.

Then Mom came in. She sat down next to me on the sofa. "I can tell you're in a bad mood," she said.

"I'm in a terrible, awful, horrible, muy mal mood," I said.

She patted my shoulder. "What's wrong?"

"Waggles drooled all over my pants. Even worse, I'm one of the only kids in third grade without any Puppet Pals."

"I can take you to the toy store today to buy some," she said.

I hugged her. "Thank you."

"You're welcome. Now get your allowance money to pay for them," Mom said.

I wished I could take back my hug. I told my mom, "I'm saving my allowance money for the *Great Epic Superhero* video game. I thought *you* would buy me Puppet Pals."

"You thought wrong," she said.

"But kids at school won't play with me unless I have Puppet Pals," I said.

"So go outside and play with the neighbors. But change your pants first," Mom said.

"Okay." I put on new pants and went outside.

My neighbors were sitting on the lawn next door. They were all playing with Puppet Pals.

I went back inside and plopped down on the couch again. I frowned again, grumbled again, and punched the pillow again. My mood was even more terrible, awful, horrible, and muy mal than before.

Then Waggles drooled on my new pants.

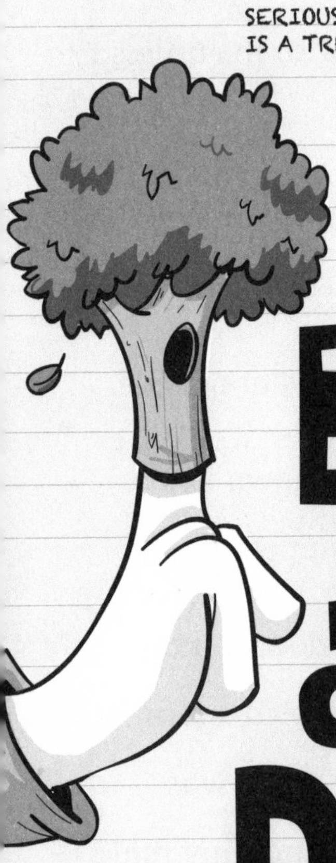

Evil in a Pink Dress

The next morning, our teacher, Mr. McNutty, held up a big cardboard clock. He moved the minute and hour hands around on it. Then he asked, "What time is it now?"

Aaron Glass raised his hand. "Time to tell time," he said.

"But what time does this fake clock show?" the teacher asked.

"Fake time," Aaron said.

Victoria Crow raised her hand. She said, "The clock shows five minutes after four o'clock." She was right as always. She's the smartest kid in third grade.

"School will be over by then, and we'll be playing with our Puppet Pals," Laurie Schneider said.

Mr. McNutty moved the clock hands again. "What time is it now?" he asked.

"A new time," Aaron Glass said.

"It is 6:53," Victoria said.

"Time to play with Puppet Pals after dinner," Owen Leach said.

"What if it was 6:53 in the morning?" the teacher asked.

"Then my mom would be telling me to get ready for school. And I'd be lying in bed, ignoring her, and playing with my Puppet Pals," Grace Chang said.

"Yeah. Me too," Emma G. said.

"Yeah. Me too," Emma J. said.

Mr. McNutty sighed. "You kids sure love those puppets. Just don't play with them in class."

Then he looked around the room. Almost everyone had Puppet Pals on their fingers. "Please put those away," he said.

"My Puppet Pal horse is galloping away," Hector Cruz said.

"My Puppet Pal race car is speeding away," Owen Leach said.

"My Puppet Pal tree is leaving. Get it? Leaving? Like leaves on a tree?" Danny Ford said.

"My Puppet Pal egg is scrambling. Get it? Scrambled eggs?" Grace Chang said.

Then Owen started singing the commercial jingle. Everyone joined in: "Puppet Pals are so much fun for just about everyone."

Mr. McNutty put his head on his desk. He seemed very tired of Puppet Pals. I put my head on my desk. I was very tired of Puppet Pals, too.

But my classmates were not tired of them. At recess, almost everyone played with Puppet Pals.

I played basketball against myself. I used my right hand to dribble and shoot. With my left hand, I tried to steal the ball away from myself. My left hand kept fouling my right hand. My left hand got benched. My right hand got injured. My right hand challenged my left hand to a fight. It was all very confusing and not much fun.

My classmates sat on the grass in a circle around Grace Chang. Grace Chang is short and tiny and usually wears frilly pink dresses. Also, she is evil. She scratched Hector with her long, scary fingernails. She made up lies about Laurie Schneider. She stuck a "Kick me" sign on my bottom. She stuck "Kick Zeke" signs on other people's bottoms. And those were just the things she did this week!

I wondered why my classmates were sitting in a circle around her.

I put the basketball away and walked over.

Grace was showing everyone her large collection of Puppet Pals. She held up a dragon puppet. "This dragon is very rare," she said. "There are only 10,000 Puppet Pal dragons in the whole world."

Everyone said, "Ooh!" or "Ahh!" or "Ooh! Ahh!" or "Ahh! Ooh!"

Everyone except me. I yawned.

Grace said, "Yuck. It's Zeke the Freak."

"Yeah. Yuck," Emma G. said.

"Yeah. Yuck," Emma J. said.

I said, "My real name is Ezekiel Heathcliff Meeks. I prefer to be called Zeke or Zeke Meeks. I do not prefer to be called Zeke the Freak."

"Grace, don't be rude to my friend," Hector said.

"That *was* pretty rude of you, Grace," Danny Ford said.

"It was rude," Aaron Glass said.

DANNY, YOU HAVE WEIRD HAIR. AARON, YOU'RE STUPID. AND ZEKE, YOU'RE A **FREAK.**

"Don't call me dumb," Aaron said.

"I didn't. I called you stupid," Grace replied.

He shrugged and said, "Oh, okay."

"Grace, you're extremely rude," I said.

"At least I'm honest," she said.

"Let's get out of here," Hector said.

Hector and I stood up and started to walk away from Grace.

A lot of kids followed us. I knew I could count on my classmates to do the right thing.

Grace said, "I have some extra Puppet Pals. I'll give them away right now to anyone who's nice to me."

Hector and I shook our heads and left.

Everyone else sat down again.

"Thanks for sticking up for me," I told Hector. "Now do you want to play basketball?"

"No thanks. I want to look at my Puppet Pals," he said.

Those Puppet Pals were ruining my life.

Hector came over to my house after school. He was carrying a box. It looked like a shoebox. He held it out and said, "Look at my new Puppet Pal Portable. It cost a lot of money, but it's worth it for my precious Puppet Pals."

I could have given him a shoebox for free.

Hector started taking his Puppet Pals out of the box.

My little sister, Mia, came over to us.

Our dog, Waggles, followed her. He was dressed in a Princess Sing-Along sweater. He looked really silly.

Mia glanced at Hector's Puppet Pals. She said, "I used to play with finger puppets a long time ago, when I was three. Now I'm too old for them."

Hector frowned. He said, "Those aren't just finger puppets. They're Puppet Pals. Zeke and I are going to play with them."

"I wanted to play basketball," I said.

"But Puppet Pals are so much fun for just about everyone," he said.

I sighed. "That's just what the commercial says. Why don't we play basketball for a half hour, and then Puppet Pals for a half hour?"

"Okay. Deal," Hector said.

"Let's shake on it," I offered.

We shook hands. Hector had Puppet Pals on most of his fingers. The vampire puppet's fangs scraped my finger.

Hector put his puppets back in the box.

Mia sang, "Toilet paper is your friend, la la la. Make sure you wipe your back end, la la la." Then she said, "Guess where I heard that song?"

"On the *Princess Sing-Along* TV show," I said.

"How did you know?" she asked.

I tapped my head. "Because I'm smart."

"And because you're wearing a Princess Sing-Along shirt, pants, and socks," Hector said.

"And because you sing Princess Sing-Along songs a hundred times a day," I said.

"That's not true," Mia said. "I sing them two hundred times a day."

"Let's get out of here," I told Hector.

We went outside and played a great basketball game.

"I forgot how much fun it was to run around," Hector said.

After a half hour, I said, "Now it's your turn, Hector. We can play with your Puppet Pals."

"Let's stay out here instead," Hector said.

"Okay." I smiled.

We played basketball for a long time.

Finally, we got so tired that we went back inside to play with Hector's Puppet Pals.

Hector took them out of his box.

"Ahh!" he screamed.

"What's wrong? Are you hurt?" I asked.

"Very hurt. My Puppet Pal vampire is missing!" he shouted. "It must have fallen off my finger when we were shaking hands. It's your fault, Zeke. You're the one who wanted to shake hands."

"It's your fault for bringing over those stupid Puppet Pals!" I shouted.

"They're not stupid!" he shouted.

"Stop shouting!" my sister Alexa shouted from her room.

"Let's just look for the missing puppet," I said.

We searched all over the living room. I didn't see the Puppet Pal vampire anywhere.

NASTY

But I did find a green moldy sandwich behind the couch. And there was a bad book report for Alexa under the couch.

I also found a ladybug on the window sill.

That made me run into my bedroom in terror.

Waggles was on my bed. Next to him were pieces of Hector's missing vampire puppet. Some pieces were still in Waggles's mouth.

YUMMY PUPPET

"I found your Puppet Pal," I called out to Hector.

"Thank you, Zeke. You're a good friend," he said as he ran into my bedroom.

When he saw the scattered pieces of his vampire puppet, he shouted, "You're not a good friend!" He ran out of my room and left my house without even saying goodbye.

I pretended my pillow was a Puppet Pal. I punched it. Then I threw it across the room. That made me feel a little better.

I went into the living room and turned on the TV to feel even better.

The Puppet Pal commercial was on.

I turned off the TV, returned to my room, and beat up my pillow again.

The next day was cold and windy. Guess what my classmates did at recess. Warmed up with a game of tag? Basketball? Four Square? Nope, nope, and nope. I bet you know what my classmates did. They sat around with their dumb Puppet Pals.

I couldn't even play basketball, because Chandler Fitzgerald was lying face down under the hoop.

He pounded his fists on the ground and cried, "It's not fair! I don't have any Puppet Pals."

I walked over to Rudy Morse.

"Hi, Zeke. What do you think is in my hand?" Rudy asked. He held out his arm to me. His hand was closed in a loose fist.

I said, "I know what's in your hand. We studied that a few weeks ago. Bones, blood cells, muscles —"

He cut me off. "I meant what I'm holding in my hand," he said.

I frowned. "A Puppet Pal?"

"No. Finger puppets are boring," Rudy said.

I smiled. "Do you have candy in your hand?"

"It's better than candy," he said.

I smiled even wider. There was only one thing better than candy. "You're holding the *Great Epic Superhero* video game! I've wanted that game for a long time. Let me see." I put my face near his hand for a close view.

He opened his hand. On his palm was a giant red beetle.

AGH!!!

"You're not scared of a cute little insect, are you?" Rudy asked.

"No. You just surprised me is all," I lied.

"Good. I found a whole bunch of beetles around the playground. This one's my favorite." Rudy stroked the beetle. I wanted to squish it.

I NAMED HIM **CUDDLES**. HE'S SO CUDDLY. DO YOU WANT TO CUDDLE HIM?

"No, thanks," I told Rudy.

"I'm trying to teach Cuddles some tricks. Shake hands, Cuddles," Rudy said. He put his finger on the giant red beetle's claw.

Suddenly, a big gust of wind blew the giant red beetle off Rudy's hand.

It landed on my arm.

Rudy said, "Aww, that's sweet. Cuddles likes you."

This was the scariest moment ever in my entire life. My jaw dropped. My skin prickled. I almost wet my pants.

"Geh-eh-eh-eh-et —" I stammered.

"What?" Rudy asked.

"Get that beetle off me!" I shouted.

So Rudy did.

I ran away.

Then I saw something almost as awful as a flying giant red beetle: flying Puppet Pals. The wind must have blown them in the air. They were going all over the place.

My classmates sat on the playground, screaming or crying. Some of them were screaming *and* crying.

"The wind!" Aaron screamed.

"Puppet Pals!" Hector cried.

"Blew away!" Owen screamed and cried.

"The wind blew away your Puppet Pals?" I asked.

"Yes!" Aaron, Hector, and Owen screamed and/or cried.

"Go get them," I said.

But no one moved. They sat on the playground, frozen, clutching the Puppet Pals they still had left. They looked like they were in shock.

So I ran around the playground collecting the Puppet Pals that had blown away. It felt good to run around at recess again. I found puppets on high tree branches, in a pile of backpacks, and deep inside Danny Ford's hair. I think I maybe found some candy, a crayon, and a quarter in his hair too.

I returned all the Puppet Pals to their owners. Everyone was happy, except for two people. Chandler Fitzgerald was still crying about not having any Puppet Pals. And Danny Ford was upset that I'd ruined his hairdo.

"Let's give a big cheer for Zeke Meeks, our hero," Hector said.

My classmates cheered for me.

Owen Leach patted me on the back.

Nicole Finkle and Buffy Maynard tried to kiss me.

"I'm sorry I got so upset about losing my Puppet Pal yesterday," Hector said.

"I'm sorry my dog ate your vampire yesterday," I said. "Do you want to play basketball?"

Hector said, "That sounds like fun —"

Owen interrupted him. He said,
"Hector, let's play with my Puppet Pal dog.
Zeke found it next to the fire hydrant. Isn't that
funny?"

"Okay," Hector said.

They walked away, leaving me alone at
recess again.

After school, I plopped down on the couch and put my head in my hands.

Mom sat next to me. "What's wrong?" she asked.

My little sister, Mia, started singing a Princess Sing-Along song. "Boys can cry. It's okay, la la la. Boys can dance in ballet, la la la. Play with dolls or wear pink clothes, la la la. Polish the nails on your toes, la la la."

"I'm not going to cry. And I don't want to dance ballet or play with dolls or wear pink clothes or polish my toenails," I said.

"I feel like crying," my older sister, Alexa, said. She came into the room holding a bunch of pencils. She said, "I spent a lot of money on these scented pencils a few years ago. They were really popular. But now they're just stinking up my bedroom."

I told Alexa, "You think you have it bad? I'm one of the only kids in third grade whose parents won't buy him any Puppet Pals."

"I'll buy you some Puppet Pals if you sweep out the basement," Mom said. "No one's been down there since your father left."

My dad is a soldier. Two months ago, he left to fight bad guys in a top-secret place. The place is so secret he can't even tell us where he is.

My dad used to exercise in the basement. But I'm scared of the basement. It's very dark down there.

I told myself to be brave like my dad. Plus, I really wanted some Puppet Pals. I told my mom, "Okay, I'll sweep the basement."

I got a broom and dustpan. Then I went down the very dark stairway to the very dark basement.

Did I mention it's very dark down there?

I felt all over the wall for the light switch. But I couldn't find it.

I don't believe in monsters.

Not usually.

But if there were monsters, very dark basements would be a good place for them. And they'd probably love to snack on eight-year-old boys.

If monsters were real.

But they aren't.

Probably.

Finally, I found the switch and turned on the light.

I looked around. The only things I saw were Dad's weights and his treadmill. No monsters.

Unless they were hiding or invisible.

But there's no such thing as monsters.

Probably.

Then I spotted something even more frightening than a monster — a moth. It flew very close to me.

I wanted to run away. But I needed to clean the basement to get Puppet Pals. So I stayed where I was.

I put my hand on the wall to steady myself so I wouldn't faint from terror. That's when I saw a terrifying spider on the wall, just a few inches from my hand.

I took my hand off the wall and put it over my mouth. Then no one could hear me scream.

I did not run away.

I started sweeping the floor.

Inches away from my foot were more terrifying insects — ants!

MY TERRIFIED LOOK

I couldn't take it anymore. I ran out of the basement and up the stairs.

I couldn't speak for a long time.

Finally I told my mom, "I changed my mind. I'm not going to sweep the basement."

"Then I won't buy you any Puppet Pals," Mom said.

I sighed. "I'll buy Puppet Pals with my allowance money."

"I thought you were saving your money for the *Great Epic Superhero* video game," she said.

"The game will have to wait," I said. I tried not to cry, even though it's okay for boys to cry.

Mom took Mia and me to the toy store.

Mia ran to the Princess Sing-Along aisle.
Pictures of Princess Sing-Along were printed
on all kinds of stuff: Dolls, sheets, towels, cups,
plates, shirts, socks, and even underwear.

She used her allowance money for a Princess
Sing-Along washcloth. She clutched it to her
chest and said, "I love this washcloth! What a
great Princess Sing-Along item for my collection!"

"You can use it during your bath tonight," I
told her.

Mia shook her head.
"Oh, no. I can't get it wet.
This Princess Sing-Along
washcloth is much too
special to actually use."

"I bet you'll get tired of Princess Sing-Along," I said.

"Never," she said.

In a few months, I thought.

Next we went to the Puppet Pals part of the toy store. It was huge and crowded. There were Puppet Pals and copycats like Felt Fingers, Finger Friends, Happy Hands, and Puppet Playmates. I saw Puppet Pal carrying cases, books, games, stickers, and underwear, too.

I chose a box of twelve Puppet Pals.

Mom peered at it and said, "That's a lot of money for bits of colored felt."

"Some of the Puppet Pals are rare and valuable," I said.

"You don't seem very excited about them," she said.

"I am." I shrugged.

"What?" she asked. "I can't hear you when you talk so quietly and dully."

"I am excited about them," I said.

"What?" Mom asked again.

"Never mind." I frowned.

We walked toward the front of the store to pay for my box of Puppet Pals and Mia's Princess Sing-Along washcloth.

On the way, I saw the *Great Epic Superhero* video game.

I stopped.

I stared at it. I touched it. I took it off the shelf.
I gave it a little hug.

It was so great and epic and superhero-ish.
I wished the kids at school liked the *Great Epic
Superhero* video game as much as they liked
Puppet Pals.

I sighed. Then I returned the video game to
the shelf. I walked to the cash register to pay for
my Puppet Pals.

I forced myself not to look back.

The box of Puppet Pals cost me most of my allowance money. It would take me a long time to save up for the *Great Epic Superhero* video game.

I still didn't feel like ballet dancing, wearing pink, playing with dolls, or polishing my toenails.

But I did feel like crying.

At recess the next day, Hector and I sat on the playground with my bag of Puppet Pals.

"This is so exciting! I can't wait to see your new puppets!" Hector exclaimed.

"Yeah," I said.

"What? I can't hear you when you talk so quietly and dully," he said.

"I'm excited," I said.

"What?" he asked again.

"Never mind." I yawned.

I pulled the Puppet Pals out of the bag one by one. First, I took out a zebra Puppet Pal.

"Zebras are cool," Hector said. "But it's too bad you didn't get the zebra with red and black stripes. That one is very rare and valuable."

Next, I pulled out a Puppet Pal that looked like a train engine.

Hector smiled and said, "Choo, choo!"

I smiled back. This was okay. But I liked basketball better.

Owen Leach came by to look at my new Puppet Pals.

Since he was so popular, a lot of kids sat down next to him.

Soon, half my class was watching me show off my Puppet Pals. They seemed more interested in the puppets than I was.

I pulled eleven Puppet Pals out of my bag. Then I said, "That's all I have. Does anyone want to play basketball?"

I'd seen the twelfth Puppet Pal yesterday. I had covered it in foil. Then I had shoved it to the bottom of the bag. I never wanted to look at it or touch it again.

I told Hector, "The twelfth Puppet Pal isn't any good." In fact, it was horrible.

"Puppet Pals are so much fun . . . ," Owen said.

The other kids joined in the commercial jingle, ". . . for just about everyone."

"Show us the last Puppet Pal," Owen ordered.

I pulled the foil out of the bag. I unwrapped the Puppet Pal and tried not to look at it. I also tried not to shake, scream, or run away.

Hector yelled, "You got the wasp Puppet Pal! That's wild!"

Was he as scared of insects as I was?

"The wasp!" Owen exclaimed.

Everyone else repeated, "The wasp!"

Victoria Crow said, "Wasps are my favorite type of insect. I love to study them. I collect wasps, too. I have wasp stuffed animals, books about wasps, wasp erasers, chocolate-covered wasps —"

TRYING NOT TO FAINT

Grace Chang interrupted her. "No one cares about that."

"Yeah. No one cares," Emma G. said.

"Yeah. No one cares," Emma J. said.

Grace went on talking. "Puppet Pal wasps are very rare. There are only 97 of them in the whole wide world. So they're worth a lot of money. That's why they're important."

"And my best friend, Zeke, has one now," Owen said.

"He's not your best friend. He's my best friend," Hector said.

"No one cares about that either," Grace said. She stood up and tried to tower over me, but she was too short to do much towering. She dangled her long, scary fingernails in front of my face. "Give me that Puppet Pal wasp or I'll rip your face off," she said.

"No." I closed my hand around the Puppet Pal.

Grace touched my cheek with her fingernail. As I said, Grace's fingernails were long and scary. They were also sharp, pointy, and (in my opinion) quite evil.

Owen glared at Grace. He said, "If you take Zeke's Puppet Pal, I'll tell everyone to never speak to you again. And they'll listen. I'm *that* popular."

Grace's long, scary, sharp, pointy, and (in my opinion) quite evil fingernail froze on my cheek.

"Owen really is that popular," I said.

"Be quiet," she said.

"Yeah. Be quiet," Emma G. said.

"Yeah. Be quiet," Emma J. said.

"You be quiet," I said.

"All three of you be quiet," Grace said.

"All four of you be quiet!" Owen said.

After Owen spoke, we quieted down. Owen really was that popular.

Then Owen said, "Grace, this is your last chance. Let Zeke go, or I'll make sure no one ever speaks to you again."

Grace frowned. She said, "Okay, you win. This time. But keep in mind that even though you are that popular, I am that evil." She took her long, scary, sharp, et cetera fingernail off my cheek. Then she giggled her evil giggle and walked away.

Emma G. and Emma J. tried to giggle evilly too. But their giggles just sounded silly. They walked away behind Grace.

I thanked Owen for sticking up for me.

He smiled. "No problem. Do you know why I rescued you from the long, scary, sharp, pointy, and, in my opinion, not-that-evil nails of Grace Chang? It's because I like you."

Wow. The most popular boy in third grade just said he liked me.

"You should come to my house and play Puppet Pals with me," he said.

Wow. The most popular boy in third grade just invited me to his house.

Owen kept smiling. "Let's be good friends," he said.

Wow. The most popular boy in third grade wanted to be good friends with me.

"Good friends share things. So you should share your Puppet Pal wasp with me," he said.

"But I just got it yesterday," I protested.

"I'll be your best friend if you give me that wasp," he said.

His mouth was smiling, but his eyes were sort of cold.

OWEN'S EYES = CREEPY!

Owen didn't wow me anymore. "Hector's my best friend," I said.

"Yeah," said Hector, "we're best friends for real, not just because we want each other's Puppet Pals." Hector smiled. His eyes were warm.

"Hey, best friend," I said. "Do you want to play basketball now?"

Hector shook his head. "No way. Now that you have your own Puppet Pals, we can play with them all the time, just like everyone else."

Not everyone was playing with Puppet Pals. I looked around the playground. Chandler was still crying. Victoria was reading a book about wasps. Rudy was training Cuddles, his giant red beetle, to roll over. But all the other third graders were playing with their Puppet Pals.

I didn't want to listen to Chandler cry, watch Victoria read about wasps, or get anywhere near Rudy's giant red beetle. So I said, "Okay, Hector. I'll play Puppet Pals with you."

I tried hard not to yawn again.

Hector and I played with our Puppet Pals every day at recess. I pretended to eat my Puppet Pal pizza. Hector made his Puppet Pal sun rise and set.

We held a battle between Hector's Puppet Pal gorilla and my Puppet Pal zebra. The gorilla won. It wasn't a fair fight. Gorillas have strong hands and feet, make scary noises, and climb and leap. Zebras just have stripes.

The more I played with Puppet Pals, the more bored I got. Instead of sitting on the playground, I would have rather played basketball, tag, or soccer. I even would have preferred to count our teacher's nose hairs. I often did that during math lectures.

Finally, I couldn't stand it anymore. I stopped pretending to change my Puppet Pal baby's diaper. I told Hector, "I don't like babies. I don't like changing diapers. And I really don't like Puppet Pals."

"But Puppet Pals are so much fun for just about everyone," Hector said. He looked confused.

"They're not much fun for me," I said.

"They're not fun for me, because I don't have any Puppet Pals," Chandler Fitzgerald sobbed.

"Chandler, you can have mine," I said. I gave him all my Puppet Pals, except the wasp.

He cried even harder.

"Now what's wrong?" I asked.

"You didn't give me your wasp," he sobbed. "And I wanted new Puppet Pals."

I rolled my eyes.

Then I walked over to Victoria. She was playing with a yo-yo that had a picture of a wasp on it.

I told her, "Since you collect wasps, I'll sell my Puppet Pal wasp to you."

She jumped up and down with excitement. After she paid me, she held the Puppet Pal wasp to her chest. "I love my new wasp!" she exclaimed. She kissed it and hugged it.

Gross.

Owen walked over to us. He stared at the Puppet Pal wasp in Victoria's loving hand. Then he said, "Victoria, you look pretty today. You always look pretty. But today you look extra pretty."

I said, "Owen, you sound phony today. You always sound phony. But today you sound extra phony."

Victoria said, "You can compliment me all you want. But you will never get my wasp Puppet Pal."

Next, Grace Chang walked up to us.

Emma G. and Emma J. followed her.

Grace put her long, scary, sharp, pointy, and evil fingernails on Victoria's cheek. "Give me the wasp Puppet Pal or I'll scratch your face off," she said.

"Yeah. Give it to her," Emma G. said.

"Yeah. Give it to her," Emma J. said.

Victoria said, "I'm the smartest kid in third grade. Therefore, you are not. Therefore, I will outsmart you. Therefore, you're toast."

"Huh? Toast?" Grace scratched her head in confusion. She must have forgotten that her fingernails were long, scary, sharp, pointy, and evil. Scratching her head made it bleed.

Emma G. and Emma J. scratched their heads, too. Their fingernails were not long, scary, sharp, et cetera like Grace's. So their heads did not bleed. But Emma J.'s barrette broke.

Victoria said, "I am the smartest kid in third grade. I understand physics and statistics. If you attempt to scratch my face off, there is a 78 percent chance that you will suffer a broken finger. There is a 46 percent chance of two or more of your fingers breaking. Think about that, Grace."

Grace thought about it. She scratched her head again. It bled again.

The Emmas scratched their heads again. Their heads did not bleed. But large flakes of dandruff fell off Emma G.'s head.

"Your head is bleeding," I told Grace.

"I'm confused, and I need a bandage," she said. She ran away.

Emma G. said, "I'm confused, and I need dandruff shampoo." She ran away, too.

Emma J. said, "I'm not confused, and I need a new barrette."

"Also, I disagree with your statistical analysis, Victoria," Emma J. continued. "You must have omitted several critical confounding factors. The chance of one finger breaking is 77 percent, and the chance of a two-finger breakage would be 45 percent." Then she ran away, too.

Victoria said, "Perhaps I'm just the second-smartest kid in third grade. But I do have the best collection of wasps."

The bell rang. Everyone lined up to return to class. Owen stood in front of me. He said, "Ha ha, Zeke. Na na na, Zeke. Nanny nanny boo boo, Zeke. You don't have any Puppet Pals now."

I told him, "The Puppet Pal fad will be over soon."

Behind me, Grace said, "It's not a fad. Puppet Pals are so much fun for just about everyone. I heard that on TV, so I know it's true."

Behind her, Emma G. said, "Yeah. It's true."

Behind her, Emma J. said, "Yeah. It's true."

I had no more Puppet Pals. Owen, the most popular boy in third grade, didn't want to be my friend. And a lot of Emma G.'s dandruff had landed on me. I felt very happy anyway.

Mr. McNutty opened the door to let us into the classroom. He said, "Remember to focus on the lessons. Don't play with your Puppet Packs."

"You mean Puppet Pals," Grace said. "Puppet Pals are so much fun . . ."

". . . for just about everyone," just about everyone in the class said.

Mr. McNutty said, "Here's a math problem. There are 60 minutes in an hour and 24 hours in a day. So how many minutes are there in a day?"

Aaron raised his hand. He said, "The answer is a lot of minutes."

Grace combed the fur of her Puppet Pal tiger. Owen squeezed the nose of his Puppet Pal clown.

I said, "Look at Grace and Owen. They know the answer."

Mr. McNutty looked at them. Just as I had hoped, he saw them playing with their Puppet Pals.

He said, "Grace Chang and Owen Leach, I told you to put those Puppet Parts away."

"Puppet Pals," Grace said.

"Well, I'm taking those Puppet Pads," our teacher said. He collected all their Puppet Pals. "You can have them back in one week," he said. "Until then, you'll pick up trash every day at recess."

I smiled. For the first time, I was grateful for Puppet Pals.

Commas Are GOOD, Comas Are BAD

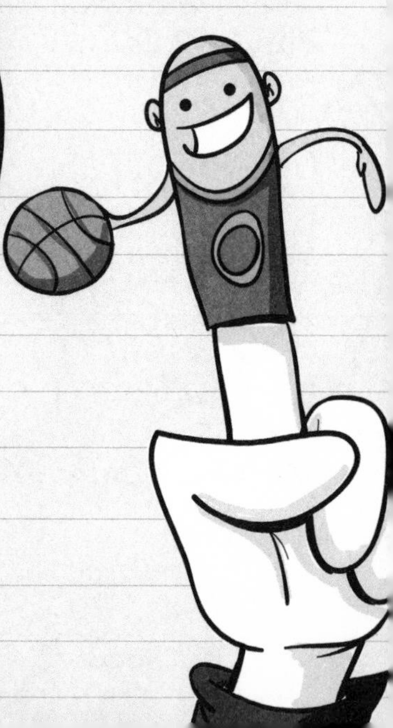

I had fun all week at recess. I practiced shooting basketballs. I taught Rudy Morse how to turn his eyelids inside out. And best of all, I watched Grace and Owen pick up trash.

The other kids played with their Puppet Pals. But they didn't seem very happy about it. When Laurie Schneider said, "Puppet Pals are so much fun," only Aaron finished the sentence. And he got it wrong. He said, "for just about anyone."

Grace told him, "It's not 'Puppet Pals are so much fun for just about anyone.' It's 'for just about everyone,' stupid."

Aaron said, "Oh, I get it now. Puppet Pals are so much fun for just about everyone stupid."

"You're stupid," Grace said.

I dropped some trash in front of her.

Hector laughed for the first time all week. "Zeke, are you sure you don't want to play with my Puppet Pals?" he asked.

They had gotten really dirty. His Puppet Pal doctor looked more like a Puppet Pal patient with an awful disease that made her pale and splotchy. Hector's Puppet Pal hamburger now looked like rotten dog food.

"I'm sure," I said.

"Sure you do or sure you don't?" he asked.

"Sure I don't," I said.

"Sure you don't what?" he asked.

"I'm sure I don't want to play with your Puppet Pals," I said.

"Are you positive?" Hector asked.

"Yes. I'm positive," I said.

"Positive about what?" he asked.

I glared at him.

"Okay. Just checking," Hector said.

Laurie started chanting again, "Puppet Pals are so much fun . . ."

Aaron joined in ". . . for just about everyone stupid."

Grace said, "It's not 'for just about everyone stupid.' It's 'for just about everyone, stupid.' There's a comma there. It's 'For just about everyone comma stupid.' Commas are important."

"My grandma was in a coma once," Aaron said.

"Comma, not coma," Grace said.

"She wasn't in a comma. She was in a coma," Aaron said.

"Now you're making me confused," Grace said. She scratched her head again. It started to bleed again.

"I'm going to play with my Puppet Pals," Aaron said.

PUPPET PALS ARE SO MUCH FUN FOR JUST ABOUT EVERYONE IN A STUPID COMA.

Hector and I laughed.

Then Hector said, "I miss playing with you, Zeke. It's not much fun playing Puppet Pals without my best friend."

"I miss playing with you, too, Hector. It's not much fun playing basketball without my best friend," I told him.

"At least you have Puppet Pals to play with. Mr. McNutty won't return mine until Monday," Grace said.

"I'll sell you my Puppet Pals," Hector offered.

"Okay," Grace said.

Soon, Hector had a lot of money in his pocket.

Grace had some old, dirty Puppet Pals on her fingers.

I had a big smile on my face.

It got even bigger when Hector and I played basketball together.

Aaron and Danny waved at us with Puppet
Pals on their fingers.

"Do you want to play basketball?" I asked.

They threw their puppets into their bags and
joined us on the court.

Then Chandler asked if he could play too.

"Of course," I said.

So he wiped away his tears and joined in
the game.

Victoria, Rudy, and Laurie played with us, too.

Owen called out, "Stop playing basketball. Puppet Pals are a lot more popular than basketball."

"I don't care about what's popular anymore," Hector said.

Grace called out, "Gather around me to see the Puppet Pals I bought from Hector."

Emma G. said, "No thanks."

Emma J. said, "No thanks."

They went to the basketball court too.

Hector said, "I'm glad I got rid of my Puppet Pals."

"Do you want to play in my backyard after school today?" I asked.

"Okay. Thanks," he said.

I smiled even bigger. I love happy endings. And I really love happy endings when they're mine.

Then I glanced at this book. I realized this isn't the ending. There are a lot more pages left. I frowned.

Everything had gone great. The Puppet Pal fad was over. My classmates were playing basketball with me. Hector had promised to play outside with me after school. And Grace and Owen were picking up trash. This was the perfect ending. So why didn't the book end here?

Because then it started to rain.

Everyone stopped playing basketball.

Chandler started crying again.

Hector said, "We won't be able to play outside after school today. Did you buy the *Great Epic Superhero* video game? That would be fun to play with."

I shook my head. "I don't have enough money for the video game."

Owen said. "Good news for Grace and me. We picked up every bit of trash. We're done."

Just my luck. Things had gone from happy to horrible in less than a page.

Then the thunder and lightning began.

A Great, Epic, Super Afternoon

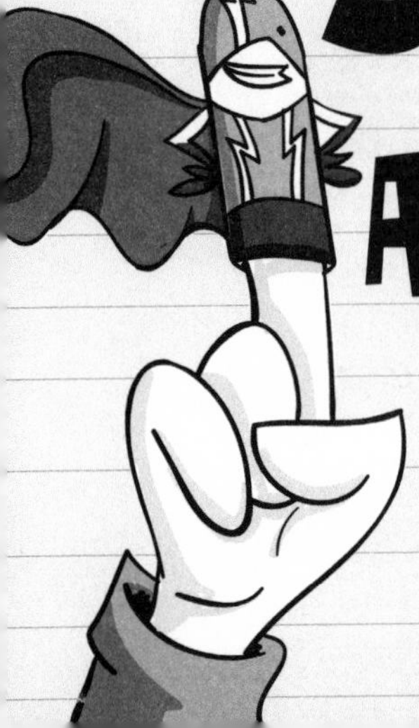

10

It was still raining when Hector came over after school.

"We'll have to think of things to do inside. We could play with my dog," I said.

Waggles was standing near us, wearing a silly pink bandana around his neck and wagging his tail.

I threw his toy bone across the room.

Waggles ran to the bone and picked it up.
Then he raced back and put the bone on my
lap. He also got a bunch of drool on my lap.

THE DOG DROOL ON YOUR
PANTS MAKES YOU LOOK LIKE
YOU HAD AN ACCIDENT.

"I know. Do you want to throw the toy
bone now?" I asked Hector. I picked up the toy.
Hanging from it was a long, thick, stretchy, and
quite disgusting string of dog drool.

Hector shook his head. "Let's watch TV instead."

"No way," Mia said. "*Princess Sing-Along* is starting. It's my favorite show."

She clicked on the TV. Then she sang along with the TV princess: "If you find it hard to hear, la la la, wax may be jammed in your ear, la la la. Don't dig out that wax yourself, la la la. Ask somebody for their help, la la la."

Mia shoved her ear in front of my eyes. "Do you see any wax in my ear?" she asked.

"No. Get away from me," I said.

Hector pointed to the TV and said, "Zeke, look at that commercial."

On TV, a bunch of kids played with bright stickers shaped like circles, ovals, squares, and stars.

A man's voice said excitedly, "Sticker Shapes! The best, newest, most popular toy for kids today. Play with them. Collect them. Bring them to school. Sticker Shapes are a joy for every girl and every boy."

"Those Sticker Shapes might become very popular. Especially if Owen Leach decides they should be popular," Hector said.

I groaned. Then I said, "I don't care how popular they become. They don't look like much fun to me. I won't buy them."

"I learned my lesson from the Puppet Pals," I added. "I'm saving my money for the *Great Epic Superhero* video game."

"That video game sounds really great and epic and super," Hector said. "I'm going to save up for it too."

"So then we can each have the same game," I said.

"Yes," Hector replied.

"After we both save our money for a long time," I said.

"Yes," Hector replied.

"And then we'll mostly play with the video game together."

"Yes," Hector replied.

"Do you see where I'm going with this?" I asked.

"No," Hector replied.

"If we each paid for half of the *Great Epic Superhero* video game, we could buy it now and share it," I said.

Hector grinned. "That's a great idea. Let's do it."

I grinned back and said, "All right!"

Finally, a perfectly happy ending.

"After we buy the video game, we can start saving for those Sticker Shapes," Hector said.

Okay, so the ending isn't perfectly happy. But it's pretty happy.

ABOUT THE AUTHOR

D. L. Green lives in California with her husband, three children, silly dog, and a big collection of rubber chickens. She loves to read, write, and joke around.

ABOUT THE ILLUSTRATOR

Josh Alves LOVES puppets! As a fan of the Muppets, he has even attempted to make his own. A constant doodler, Josh eventually grew up, married an incredible woman, and gets to draw with his three kids in his studio in Maine.

DO YOU LIKE TO SIT AROUND AT RECESS?
(And other really important questions)

Write answers to these questions, or discuss them with your friends and classmates.

1. Do you like to sit around at recess? If so, WHY!? What is your favorite thing to do at recess?

2. Let's say all of your friends loved a certain new toy, but you thought it was lame. Would you buy it anyway?

3. Hector was so mad when Zeke's dog destroyed his Puppet Pal. Was that fair? Has something similar ever happened between you and your friends?

4. The Puppet Pal jingle got stuck in everyone's heads. Write your own jingle for this book. Can you make it as catchy as the Puppet Pal one?

BIG WORDS
according to Zeke

TRY USING THEM IN SENTENCES JUST LIKE I DO

ALLOWANCE: The money you get from your parents, usually for helping out around the house. People like Grace Chang probably don't have to do anything for their allowance.

COMA: If you are in a coma, you are sleeping and no one can wake you up, no matter what. You are also probably sick or hurt.

COMMERCIALS: Things that interrupt your TV shows and try to get you to bug your parents into buying you something that you may or may not need.

COMPLIMENT: To say nice things about someone. It makes them feel all warm and fuzzy and nice inside.

DANDRUFF: Yucky, white, flaky stuff that comes off people's scalps.

DISEASE: Something awful that makes people feel sick and tired.

DISGUSTING: Things that make you go, "EW!" like Princess Sing-Along, most girls, and every bug known to man.

EARWIG: Possibly the worst and, therefore, most disgusting bug ever, thanks to its superlong antennae and clawlike end.

GRRRRR!

ET CETERA: A phrase you say when you want people to know you could keep on listing things but you think they may already be tired of your already long list.

EXTREMELY: Super-duper, very much so.

INDEX FINGER: The finger you use to point at things. Also, the most popular finger for your Puppet Pals, according to some people.

JINGLE: The catchy tunes in commercials that get stuck in your brain, refusing to leave.

MOLDY: Rotten and covered with green-and-white fur.

PHYSICS AND STATISTICS: Two really hard subjects you probably won't learn until college, unless you are the smartest kid in the third grade.

PRICKLED: Felt stingy and tingly all over. This could be a good feeling or a bad feeling, depending on what caused it.

RIDICULOUS: Very silly and just not right, like Waggles in girly clothes.

WAITING LIST: A list of names of people who are waiting for something. Just sitting around waiting. Doing nothing but waiting.

Make Your Own Puppet Pal

If you wanted to have a Puppet Pal of your own — I have no idea why you would — but if you did, you could make one. Here are some step-by-step directions for a boring bird. Er, I mean, a bird that will be fun for just about everyone!

What you need:

- felt pieces; use bright, crazy colors for best results

- craft scissors

- craft glue

- googly eyes

- craft feathers

SUPER Z TO THE RESCUE

What you do:

1. Cut two rectangles from the felt. Each should measure 1 5/8 inches x 3 inches. Round the top corners to create a head shape on one end.

2. Glue the pieces together on three sides, leaving an opening for your finger on the flat bottom.

3. For a beak, cut a small triangle from the felt. Use the same color or a different one. It is your choice! Glue your beak on.

4. Glue on googly eyes. Then add a feather to each side for wings, and a small feather on top of the head. Make sure you let it all dry before you play with it.

SAY YOUR GOODBYES, DOG SLAYER!

SOCKS?

Still don't have enough Puppet Pals?

Download printable paper pals, part of a Zeke Meeks activity kit, at **capstonekids.com/characters/Zeke-Meeks**

WWW.CAPSTONEKIDS.COM